DANGEROUS GAMES

THE NIGHTMARE KNIGHT

Sue Graves

D1301752

RISING STARS

Rising Stars UK Ltd.
7 Hatchers Mews, Bermondsey Street, London SE1 3GS
www.risingstars-uk.com

nasen

NASEN House, 4/5 Amber Business Village, Amber Close,
Amington, Tamworth, Staffordshire B77 4RP

Published 2012

Author: Sue Graves
Series editor: Sasha Morton
Text and logo design: pentacor**big**
Typesetting: Geoff Rayner, Bag of Badgers
Cover design: Lon Chan
Publisher: Gill Budgell
Project Manager: Sasha Morton Creative Project Management
Editorial: Deborah Kespert
Artwork: Colour: Lon Chan / B&W: Paul Loudon

British Library Cataloguing in Publication Data.
A CIP record for this book is available from the British Library.

ISBN: 978-0-85769-612-0

Printed by Craftprint International, Singapore

It was Tuesday morning and Kojo was late for work … again! Sima and Tom were feeling worried.

Sima, Tom and Kojo worked at Dangerous Games, a computer games company. Sima designed the games, Kojo programmed them and Tom tested them. They worked as a team and they all loved their jobs. The three of them were best mates, too.

Just then, Kojo rushed in. He sat down and rubbed his eyes wearily.

"Morning, Kojo," said Tom. "What have you been up to? This is the third day running that you've been late."

"You don't look well," said Sima. "Are you ill?"

Kojo shook his head. "No, I'm not ill," he said. "But I keep having the same nightmare. I had it again last night, it was awful. I woke up in a sweat and I still feel weird now."

"Did you have cheese before you went to sleep?" asked Sima. "I've heard that eating cheese before bedtime can give you nightmares."

"That's nonsense," said Tom. "I love cheese. I eat it all the time and I never have nightmares. Kojo's just got a vivid imagination, that's all."

Kojo looked miserable. "Worse still, I've just bumped into Janet Winter and she wants to have a word with me later on in the week."

"Poor you, having 'a word' with Janet never ends well," sighed Tom. "I should know."

CHAPTER 2

Tom, Sima and Kojo got on with their work, but Kojo was miserable all morning. At lunchtime, Sima and Tom tried to cheer Kojo up.

"Tell us about your nightmare," said Sima.

"It's really grim," Kojo explained. "I'm in this massive castle in medieval times and I have to joust with a knight."

"But that sounds cool," interrupted Tom.

"It gets worse than that," said Kojo. "As the joust goes on, the knight becomes more ferocious and I can hardly stay on my horse." Kojo shuddered. "The knight knocks me off my horse with his lance and then strides over and holds a sword to my throat. But when he takes off his helmet, he hasn't got a face. In fact, there's nothing inside the armour at all. No head, no body, nothing. I haven't been fighting anything, just some unseen force. That's when I wake up."

"That's not scary! You need to toughen up, Kojo," retorted Tom.

All afternoon, Tom teased Kojo about his nightmare. He put his jacket over his head and pretended he was headless. Kojo didn't think it was funny at all.

"Just give it a rest!" grumbled Kojo.

Then, Sima had a good idea. "Why don't we use Kojo's nightmare as the basis for a new computer game?" she suggested. "We haven't done a historical game before. Two players could each control a knight in a jousting tournament."

"That sounds OK," agreed Kojo, "just so long as we don't have any headless knights. Or knights with no bodies at all!" He shuddered again at the memory of his nightmare.

"But that would make the game more exciting!" said Tom.

"No way," interrupted Kojo. "I'll only program the game if the knights all have bodies and heads!"

"OK," said Sima. "I'll get to work on the designs, but I think it might be a bit boring."

CHAPTER 3

The next day, the designs were ready and Kojo programmed the game. He had it done in no time at all.

"What are we going to call this game?" asked Sima.

"Battling Knights?" suggested Kojo.

"*Boring* Battling Knights might be a better name," moaned Tom. Kojo looked hurt.

"Perhaps we'll leave the name for now," said Sima. "I'm sure we'll think of something later." She smiled kindly at Kojo. "But I think this might be a good game to test for real. It wouldn't be dangerous."

"No, that's what worries me," Tom muttered under his breath.

By the end of the week, the game was ready for testing.

"We'll test it this evening," said Tom, "after work as usual. OK?"

"OK," said Kojo and Sima.

Just then the phone rang. It was Janet Winter. She wanted to see Kojo in her office right away.

"Oh dear," said Kojo when he put down the phone. "I've been dreading this."

He hurried out of the office. As soon as the door had closed, Tom sat down at Kojo's computer.

"What are you up to?" asked Sima looking over Tom's shoulder.

"I thought we could adjust the game a little to make it more exciting," replied Tom.

"You can't do that," said Sima. "Kojo will be furious if he finds out you've tampered with the program."

"He won't find out," said Tom. "I just want to make the knights fiercer and the jousts more exciting, that's all."

"I don't know if we should," said Sima. She looked worried.

"Leave it to me," said Tom. "It will make all the difference."

"OK," said Sima. "But don't add any headless knights or anything, will you?"

But Tom wasn't listening. He was too busy tweaking the program to reply.

Sima picked up her bag. "I'm going for a coffee," she sighed. "I'll see you later."

That evening, when everyone else had gone home, Sima, Tom and Kojo got ready to test the game.

"Let's just remind ourselves of the rules," said Kojo as he loaded the game onto his computer. "Remember, we all have to touch the screen together to enter the game. And the game is only over when we hear the words 'Game Over'. Is that clear?"

Sima and Tom nodded.

"OK," said Kojo. "Let's enter the game."

Tom, Sima and Kojo touched the screen. A bright light flashed and they squeezed their eyes shut.

CHAPTER 4

The bright light faded and Tom, Sima and Kojo opened their eyes. They were in the courtyard of a medieval castle, wearing clothing from that time.

WOW, LOOK AT ME! I LOOK LIKE A MEDIEVAL PEASANT. HOW DID THAT HAPPEN?

Tom looked at Kojo. "Hey, how come you get to wear the armour?"

"I have no idea," said Kojo. "But I'm beginning to feel worried already."

"Don't worry, mate," said Tom. "This is going to be brilliant."

Just then a teenage boy came up to them. He was leading a horse on reins.

"Excuse me, sire," said the boy to Kojo. "The joust is about to start."

"Excuse me?" said Kojo. "Who are you?"

"I am Max, the stablehand. I look after all of your horses," he replied. "Sire, everyone is in the arena. You must mount your horse, now."

"But I can't ride," spluttered Kojo.

The boy roared with laughter and said, "You jest, sire. You are the best rider in the kingdom. I should know."

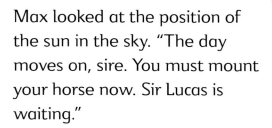

Max looked at the position of the sun in the sky. "The day moves on, sire. You must mount your horse now. Sir Lucas is waiting."

Kojo swallowed hard and mounted the horse. The ground looked a long way down and he shut his eyes. "I thought we controlled the knights in the joust, Sima. You never said anything about actually jousting ourselves."

Sima looked concerned. "Yes, you're just supposed to control the knight. I don't understand it," she said.

GOOD LUCK, KOJO!

Max led Kojo to an arena just outside the castle walls. A large crowd of people were waiting excitedly for the tournament to begin. At one end of the arena was a raised platform where a king and queen sat on large thrones. Trumpeters stood to attention next to them. At the other end was a knight on a black horse. The horse was stamping the ground and snorting impatiently.

Max handed Kojo a lance.

IS THAT SIR LUCAS?

YES, SIRE, THAT IS SIR LUCAS.

33:00

Just then, the trumpeters sounded a fanfare and the crowd fell silent. The king slowly raised his arm. He was holding a gauntlet. The crowd watched and waited, then the king dropped the gauntlet. The crowd roared with excitement. Sir Lucas's horse reared up and galloped at top speed towards Kojo.

Kojo's horse sprang forward and galloped towards Sir Lucas.

WOW, I REALLY CAN RIDE! THIS IS AMAZING.

Kojo saw Sir Lucas aim his lance as the two horses drew level. Kojo tried to balance his own lance but it was tricky to hold. Sir Lucas crashed his lance into Kojo. Kojo slipped in his saddle but managed to hang on. The horses turned and Sir Lucas charged again — this time Kojo was ready. He caught the knight full in the chest and Sir Lucas fell to the ground.

"Hurray!" cheered the crowd.

Kojo turned in his saddle and gave Sima and Tom the thumbs up.

"That was easy," he called. "Sir Lucas won't get up again in a hurry."

LOOK OUT, KOJO! THE KNIGHT'S BACK ON HIS FEET.

Sir Lucas was sitting on his horse in exactly the same place as before. The horse was stamping the ground and snorting impatiently.

"How weird," said Kojo.

Just then Max appeared. He looked at the position of the sun in the sky and spoke to Kojo. "The day moves on, sire. Sir Lucas is waiting to joust with you."

16:00

Before Kojo knew what was happening, he was galloping towards Sir Lucas. Once again, he found it tricky to balance his lance and Sir Lucas nearly knocked him from his saddle. The horses turned and Sir Lucas charged again. As before, Kojo caught him full in the chest with his lance and Sir Lucas fell to the ground.

The crowd cheered. But then, straight away, Sir Lucas appeared in the same place as before and was once more galloping on his horse towards Kojo. The joust played out exactly as it had before.

"What's happening?" said Sima. "I've never seen anything like it."

Then Sima remembered something. She glared at Tom. "What did you do to the program this afternoon?"

Tom went red. "I'm so sorry," he said. "I think I must have messed it up when I was tweaking it. I was only trying to spice up the game a bit."

"Spice it up!" shouted Sima. "Kojo is stuck in a game that he can't get out of. Worse still, the game time is stuck as well. We're never going to get out of here!"

"Let me think," said Tom. "We've got to break the game cycle in some way."

"But how?" said Sima. She looked at Kojo as once more he jousted with Sir Lucas. "I don't think Kojo can last much longer, he looks exhausted."

CHAPTER 5

Kojo was at the start of the joust yet again. Sweat was pouring off him and he felt sick with tiredness. His horse began to gallop towards Sir Lucas and he held on tightly to the lance. It felt heavier and heavier as he tried to aim it at the knight.

Then, just as Sir Lucas and Kojo drew level, Sima and Tom threw lots of shiny pebbles on the ground in front of Sir Lucas's horse. The horse's hooves began to slip and slide on the pebbles and Sir Lucas was thrown into the air. He hit the ground with a sickening crunch. The knight moaned and then lay still. A gasp went up from the crowd.

Tom threw a heavy sword to Kojo. "Catch!" he shouted. Kojo caught the sword.

"Behead the knight quickly," yelled Tom.

"You're kidding!" cried Kojo. "I can't do that."

"You must, Kojo, or else we will all be stuck in the game forever," shouted Tom.

Kojo swung the sword above his head. But Sir Lucas rolled over and sprang to his feet. He stretched out his arm and pointed his finger at Kojo. Kojo stared open-mouthed as a huge sword appeared from nowhere in the knight's hand. Sir Lucas swished the sword through the air and, with a roar of anger, ran at Kojo. Kojo fell backwards and the knight pressed the sword into his neck.

Kojo kicked out at the knight and sent him sprawling on the ground.

QUICKLY, KOJO! BEHEAD HIM NOW, BEFORE IT'S TOO LATE.

Using every last bit of his strength, Kojo swung the sword high above his head and, closing his eyes, brought it down hard across Sir Lucas's neck. The helmet rolled away from the knight's body and spun round and round on the ground. A great cheer rose from the crowd.

Using the point of his sword, Kojo flicked open the helmet's visor. Then he gasped and sank to his knees. Tom and Sima ran to help him. Kojo was shaking from head to foot.

"Kojo, you won!" exclaimed Sima. "The game time is about to run out at last. What's the matter? Are you injured?"

"No," whispered Kojo. He pointed at the helmet still spinning on the ground. "Look! It's like in my nightmare. I've been fighting a headless knight."

Just then a bright light flashed and Sima, Tom and Kojo shut their eyes tightly as they heard the words 'Game Over'.

The light faded and Sima, Kojo and Tom opened their eyes. They were back in the office.

"Right, Tom," said Kojo angrily. "I want to know why that game was such a disaster. I guess you were behind this mess in some way?"

"I don't know what you mean," said Tom, shifting uncomfortably from foot to foot.

"Oh yes you do," said Sima. "You tell Kojo what you did."

"I only tweaked the game a little," said Tom. "I thought it would make it more exciting."

"By messing around with the program you introduced a virus. The virus corrupted the program and altered the way the game was meant to be played. I was lucky to survive," said Kojo.

"Tom is really sorry, aren't you?" said Sima. "And he did work out how to break the cycle so we could get out."

"Sima's right," said Tom. He patted Kojo on the shoulder. "I'm really sorry you had such a hard time in the game. I won't interfere with your programming again."

"And maybe now you've defeated the knight in real life, you won't meet him in your nightmare again!" said Sima, trying to cheer Kojo up. "No more tiredness or being late for work."

"No more Janet Winter!" said Tom and Kojo at the same time. They both laughed.

"I've even got the perfect name for the game," said Tom, as they got ready to leave the office.

"You have?" said Kojo.

"Yes," said Tom. "Let's call it Knightmare!"

"Knightmare! Now why didn't I think of that?" said Kojo, rolling his eyes.

Glossary of terms

arena a large area used for sports or entertainment

armour metal clothing that soldiers wore in medieval times

courtyard a square outdoor area that is surrounded by walls or buildings

fanfare a short, loud piece of music played to announce an event

gauntlet a thick heavy glove

jest to joke

joust a fight on horseback between two knights who use lances to try and hit each other

kingdom a country or an area that is ruled over by a king or queen

knight long ago, a knight was a soldier who wore a suit of armour and rode a horse

lance a long pointed weapon

medieval a period in European history between about 1000 AD and 1500 AD

rein(s) long straps used to control a horse

tamper(ed) to interfere with something and change it

tournament a sporting event from the past

vivid If you have a vivid imagination you can imagine pictures in your mind easily

Quiz

1 Why was Kojo late for work?

2 Who wanted to see him later in the week?

3 In what period of history was the game set?

4 What was the name of the boy who led Kojo's horse?

5 What did the king drop to start the joust?

6 What was the name of the knight Kojo had to fight?

7 What did Tom and Sima throw under the horse?

8 What did Tom throw to Kojo?

9 What did Tom tell Kojo to do?

10 What did the crowd do at the end?